- DON'T BE LATE!
- THE ADVENTURE IS
- ABOUT TO START!!

Alice's

ADVENTURES

ON THE LONDON

UNDERGROUND

PETER LAWRENCE

illustrated with wood engravings by

Andrew Davidson

For Ada, Iris, Elliot,
Mavis and Dulcie

First published in 2023 by
Signal Books Limited
36 Minster Road
Oxford OX4 1LY
www.signalbooks.co.uk

Design and text © Peter Lawrence 2023
Illustrations © Andrew Davidson 2023

A catalogue record for this book is available from the British Library.

ISBN 978-1-8384630-8-3 Paper

Production by Tora Kelly
Printed in India by Imprint Press

Preamble

Charles Dodgson was brought up at Croft-on-Tees, just four miles from the Stockton-Darlington railway, the first commercial trainline in Britain. As a child he devised a railway game for his brothers and sisters to play with 'stations' placed around the garden. The 'train' was made from a wheelbarrow, a barrel and a small truck. He always enjoyed travelling on trains and as an adult, we know he owned a copy of the famous Bradshaw timetables.

In July 1862, on a river trip in Oxford, Dodgson told a story to Alice Liddell. When Alice asked him to write the story down, he agreed, and in 1864, he presented his hand-written version to her, which he called *Alice's Adventures Under Ground*. Only later did the published edition become *Alice's Adventures in Wonderland* under the name Lewis Carroll.

Going underground was a topic of the time. The first underground railway in the world was opened in London in 1863. It ran from Paddington (the London station at which Dodgson regularly arrived from Oxford) through King's Cross to Farringdon. Did Dodgson ever travel on the new Underground steam trains? Almost certainly.

What tales did he tell to child passengers on his train journeys? We can only imagine… such as a story he told about the Wonderland characters visiting London and waiting for Alice to join them. That must have been an interesting tale. A great pity they arrived at Paddington before he could finish it. I wonder how the story would have ended…

Contents

All in the golden afternoon
We fools, we push and shove,
The shoppers and the business suits
Leave world and sky above,
But one will dream of flights of fancy,
Not of raven, but of dove.

Alice! A new child's story's made,
And with imagination,
Twisting Carroll's fantastic tale,
Through a tunnel of creation.
Keep childhood in your memory bank,
Make love your destination.

TRACK ONE

Down the escalator

It was a cool July day and a clock was striking three. A young girl was tired of window-shopping with her older sisters on a crowded Oxford Street. They had come to London from Oxford for the day to help her spend her birthday money. She'd been looking forward to it. She'd never been to London before. The day started off thrillingly, going on her first big red London bus from Paddington to Oxford Street. But the shopping was rather disappointing. She hadn't bought anything. It looked like it might not be an exciting day-trip after all. 'What is the point of shops selling things that aren't beautiful or useful?' the young girl said out loud. 'And that we can't afford anyway.' Her mind began to wander. She was just thinking she'd rather be back home, sitting by a peaceful river bank having a picnic, when a white rabbit ran past her, muttering to itself 'Oh dear! Oh dear! It's three o'clock already. I shall be too late!' He was looking at a watch, taken from his waistcoat pocket and at a timetable pulled from his jacket. He ran past her and on down the street. The girl thought how odd this was – 'you don't see many pocket watches these days' she said to herself, and before she knew it, she was chasing after the rabbit just in time to see it disappear down the steps of Oxford Circus Underground station. Not thinking what she was doing, she ran down after it. 'Oh, I like a good circus' she thought, but was disappointed not to see any jugglers or clowns in this huge space below the street. There was only a uniformed man with a walrus moustache. 'Come on, hurry up, you'll need an Oyster card!' the rabbit called out to her as he was running and grabbed one from the Walrus man as they passed. The girl was sure she heard her Oyster speak:

'Thank you, thanks for saving us,
we thought we would be eaten.
We tried to tell them more than once,
we didn't have much meat on.
Thank you, thanks for saving us,
those guards they must be beaten.'

They sped through the barrier to the top of some odd-looking stairs that stretched down… and down. So far down she couldn't see where they ended.

The rabbit stopped. He looked nervously at his watch. The girl stopped behind him. 'Why do you keep looking at your watch?' she enquired. 'Well, you don't know much do you?' replied the rabbit. 'It wouldn't be a watch if I didn't keep watching it.' The stairs were moving. 'How unusual' she thought. 'My stairs at home never move. I mean, how would I ever get upstairs if the stairs were always moving down?' She tried to work out if she could run up the stairs faster than they were coming down. 'Fancy having to run fast just to stay in the same place' she thought.

'If you're in a hurry, why aren't we running down the stairs?' she asked. 'Because if you want to catch a train, you must keep stationary' said the rabbit. The girl laughed. 'Standing still and moving at the same time, how very peculiar.' 'Not peculiar at all,' replied the rabbit. 'Standing and running can be the same thing you know. Haven't you ever heard of people who stand for election, whereas others run for office?' The girl gave this some thought but it made her giddy and she decided that it was not a good idea to feel dizzy on moving stairs.

She strained her eyes but couldn't see right to the bottom. 'Why are you staring?' asked the rabbit. 'Stairs don't like being stared at you know.' She was going to argue but looked instead to the sides of the escalator and noticed there were pictures in frames. One was of a jar of honey. It looked so real. 'That would be nice for tea' she thought, but try as she might she couldn't grab hold of the jar.

Down, down, down they went. Would these stairs never end? She felt she was floating. Finally they reached the bottom. 'Hooray!' shouted the girl. 'Hurry!' shouted the rabbit, looking at his timetable. 'We want the Victoria Line. The train is due any second!' and he bounded off down a long corridor. 'Victoria?' she thought. 'She was a Queen, so I suppose this must be her train.' The girl was good at history and knew all the Kings and Queens of England. She knew that Victoria reigned a lot in Britain. 'But then, it always rains a lot in Britain' she thought and giggled. 'Is it the Queen's train?' she asked the rabbit when she caught him up. 'No, of course not' said the rabbit. 'The trainline was just named after her.' 'Well, they could hardly have named it before her' she thought. 'So, the Queen doesn't have her own train?' 'She did once' said the rabbit, 'when she got married – it was attached to her dress.'

The rabbit was becoming agitated. 'Oh my ears and whiskers, how late it's getting!' The station was busy with people hurrying in all directions – business people, shoppers, tourists everywhere. The young girl chased after the rabbit and on to a platform just as an Underground train came speeding out of the tunnel. 'This is not like any train I've seen before,' she thought. It stopped and as if by magic, the doors opened. 'Mind the gap!' shouted the rabbit.

TRACK TWO

Oxford Circus to Warren Street

'We made it!' exclaimed the rabbit jumping onto the train and swinging himself around a pole in delight. 'But where are we going?' said the girl as the doors closed behind them. 'We are just going one stop,' said the rabbit. The girl was even more confused. 'How can you "go" a "stop"?' She sat herself down on a seat and looked around. The small voice in her head said 'I can see two dozing people.' 'Don't you mean "two dozen"?' 'No' the voice whispered back. 'Two of them are asleep.'

The rabbit was a familiar sight to the passengers. No one in the carriage said a word and apparently nobody thought a rabbit wearing a waistcoat with a pocket watch was in any way unusual. She looked out of the window. All was black. 'How boring' she thought.

'I'll never complain about the view from my bedroom window ever again.' She looked up above the seats opposite. There were some advertisements on the wall above the windows. One was for a café called *Drink Me! Eat Me!* with pictures of a bottle of lemonade and a cupcake. 'They look nice.' Above that was a funny kind of map. 'I like maps' she thought, 'but this is very dull. It's just a straight line with names.'

She was thinking what an odd day she was having when the rabbit jumped up. A voice sounded as if from nowhere. *'The next stop is Warren Street — mind the gap!'* 'Here we are — home' he said. The young girl looked puzzled. 'Rabbits live in warrens — I thought you'd know that.'

No sooner had they stepped off the train onto Warren Street station, than the rabbit was running again, down a long corridor. The girl decided she was tired of running and just watched as the rabbit disappeared into the distance.

'Slow down!' shouted the girl 'or you'll…' Suddenly, the rabbit went head over paws. '…or you'll fall over.' 'I hope he enjoyed the trip' said the voice in her head. She

looked around her. Where was she? On the platform wall was a maze made out of tiles. She sat down on the seat beneath the maze. 'You could say that this looks *amazing*' said the small voice in her head. 'No I won't!' she replied.

Just as she was thinking that the rabbit had been gone a long time, and that maybe she was dreaming and it didn't really exist, the white rabbit reappeared wearing white gloves and dressed in a green jacket with a large GWR badge on the lapel. 'Nice uniform' she said. 'It's my tracksuit' he chuckled. 'Well, you look very smart, but you seem taller than before.' 'That will be my platform shoes' whispered the rabbit.

'Excuse me Mr Rabbit?' (She thought she ought to address him more formally now he was in uniform.) 'Have we met before? You seem familiar.' But Rabbit was busy, feeling in his pockets, looking at his watch and checking his phone.

A small group of people had gathered on the platform alongside the girl. She wondered what was going to happen next. The rabbit cleared his throat, stood to attention and spoke in an important sounding voice.

'Welcome everyone. My name is…' Then he paused. He looked around. In fact he swizzled round three times. He swizzled so fast that his head became quite dizzy and swozzled.

'My name is… White Rabbit!' 'Well, I could have guessed that!' said the girl, very unimpressed. The rabbit continued. 'Gather round. Welcome to the three o'clock GWR – Great White Rabbit – tour of the London Underground. I'll be your guide today for your tip-top tour of tunnels, trains and tales of the Tube – the oldest underground railway network in the world.' He did a little tap dance, spread his arms out wide and declared 'While you take the train… let Rabbit take the strain.'

He took some folded pieces of paper from his inside pocket and handed one to each person. 'This,' he said, 'is your Underground map to keep. You can use it to follow our route through the subterranean world under London.' 'Subter…what?' thought the girl. White Rabbit carried on. 'Subterranean means under the ground' he explained, as if he'd heard what she was thinking. 'It shows you all the stations with all the routes in different colours.'

'I wonder how you learn to be a Guide on the Underground?' said the voice in the girl's head. Once again, it was as if the White Rabbit had heard her. 'In case you were wondering... I had to *train* for this job.' The rabbit giggled and doubled up, holding his tummy with laughter. 'You shouldn't laugh at your own puns' said the girl sternly. 'You shouldn't pun-ish me for laughing' replied the rabbit. 'It's no joke being funny, you know.'

'I know a joke, I know a joke...' said the small voice in the girl's head. 'For goodness sake hurry up and tell us then' replied the girl in a whisper. Rabbit turned towards her looking cross. 'I'll go as hurriful or slowlified as I please, young lady' he said. 'Sorry Mr Rabbit' said the girl. 'I was just talking to myself. I didn't realize you could hear me.' 'What, with *these* ears!' said the rabbit, and he laughed again, holding his sides. The girl began, 'Well, here's my joke. Question: Where are whales weighed?' 'That's too easy!' laughed the rabbit. 'But we've no time for jokes now. Maybe later. Much later.'

The rabbit composed himself and turned to look at the very large map on the wall. 'We are here' he said to the group, pointing to Warren Street. He spoke in a very boring voice… 'the train lines are coded in colour on the map. We will travel first on the light blue Victoria Line towards King's Cross. You see, the line starts all the way down at Brixton in the south. King's Cross station was on the very first Underground line, run by the Metropolitan Railway which linked the centre of London with Brunel's Great Western Railway at Paddington.'

Rabbit began tracing the blue line with his gloved finger. 'Stockwell, Vauxhall, Pimlico, Victoria, Green Park, Oxford Circus, Warren Street, Euston, King's Cross…' The girl was bored. 'Will this never end!?' she said out loud. 'Of course it will' said the rabbit, 'at Walthamstow Central.' She looked at her map. 'What's after Walthamstow Central?' she asked. 'Nothing,' said the rabbit. 'Walthamstow is the end of the Underground world. But see… there's also the brown line from Elephant & Castle to Harrow. The red line from Epping to West Ruislip. The green line from Richmond to Upminster. The black line from High Barnet to Morden. The dark blue line from Uxbridge to Cockfosters.' 'And what's after Cockfosters?' she asked. 'Absolutely nothing' said the rabbit. 'But isn't it a brilliant map?' She had to agree.

The young girl was already thinking that this was a day like no other – a talking rabbit; a moving staircase; a funny train… and a lecture on the history of the London Underground. All very odd. But that was nothing to what was to happen next.

'How long does the tour last?' said the girl. 'I think someone might miss me.' 'Oh, don't worry, you'll be back here in no time' said the rabbit. 'No time at all.' A train appeared out of the tunnel. 'Wait here please, behind the yellow line till the train stops,' said White Rabbit to the group in his 'important' voice. 'And mind the gap!'

TRACK THREE

All change!

As the train came to a stop, the girl had a start! She just had a second to glimpse her reflection in the doors before they slid open… 'Is that *me*?' she thought. The doors opened. Rabbit jumped on followed by the others. But as the girl stepped onto the train, she suddenly felt very odd. She hesitated. 'Come on young lady,' called the rabbit holding out his hand to help her. 'Jump on.' The girl had put one foot into the carriage. It was as if… everything went into slow motion. 'This… feels… like… walking… through… treacle' she thought (not that she'd ever walked through treacle).

White Rabbit piped up 'Please hurry up now… one small step for a girl, one giant leap for Girlkind.' She was now on the train. The doors closed. Something was definitely different. She felt strange. Everything felt really weird…. She turned and caught sight of her reflection in the glass in the train doors. There was a girl, looking back at her. 'How odd,' she thought. 'It looks like me, but she's wearing a dress. When I left Oxford this morning I'm sure I was wearing my new jacket and skirt that I had for my birthday… at least I think I was.' It was all very puzzling. 'And her hair is long and blonde – mine's long and brown.' She smiled. The girl looking back at her smiled. She pulled a funny face and did a dance. The girl did the same. She stepped forward to touch the glass. The girl in the reflection held out her hand to meet hers. As their fingers touched she felt as if a wave had run through her. 'Like when we lay on the beach,' she thought 'and let the water wash over us.'

She looked down. She was pleased to see that she was still wearing her own clothes. She looked at her reflection. There she was again… wearing a dress. 'How very peculiar' she thought. 'I shall never look at a mirror in the same way again.' She turned to the rabbit. How curious. He now seemed even more familiar. And, looking along the carriage, there were no longer any people on the train.

Instead, the tour party was now made up of some very strange creatures – a couple of eaglets; a duck; a parrot; a turtle; a mouse and a dodo. 'Curiouser and curiouser' she thought. 'A real live dodo?! I can't wait to tell them back in the museum in Oxford.' She took one more look at her other self in the mirror. 'I've seen that girl before…'.

The White Rabbit was now looking shocked himself. His white face had turned even whiter. He'd seen her reflection too and was now looking at this girl on the train as if for the first time. If he'd opened his eyes any wider, they would have popped out of his head. He could hardly speak. In his mind there flashed a picture of another White Rabbit wearing a waistcoat and holding a pocket watch – a faded picture from some distant family memory. 'Have we met before?' he stuttered, trembling. 'I asked *you* first, ten minutes ago' said the girl, rather crossly. The White Rabbit was just about to ask the girl's name when the dodo spoke up.

'What fun! Let's play the name game!' said Dodo. 'We'll all say names starting from A and going on to Z and see who gets her name right first. For every name we guess wrong we lose points. The quicker we guess it, the more bonus points we get for saving time.' 'How do you save time?' interrupted the girl. 'Is it like saving money? My sisters and I save ours in a piggy-bank.' 'So do... do... I' said Dodo. 'I save hours in a piggy-bank, and minutes in a jam jar.' 'I save my money in the River Bank' added the duck. 'I save cheese by...' started the mouse. 'Will you please all save your breath!?' snapped the rabbit.

He took a deep breath himself. He was trying to calm down. Had he really seen what he thought he'd seen in the reflection? 'What *would* save time, young lady, is if your name started with a letter near the front of the alphabet. I know it's not likely but... is there any hope... even the slightest possibility that your name starts with... an A?'

'I don't know', said the girl. 'I'm a bit muddled up. My name is... oh dear, I really am confused.' By now, her head was spinning. 'If I remember my geometry lessons correctly,' she thought, 'this going round in circles has something to do with Sir Cumference. Whoever he was.' The voice in her head said 'when it stops turning, I hope it finishes face front. People say "you need eyes in the back of your head", but I'd rather not. I wouldn't know if I was coming or going.' She looked around at the group of funny characters. They were all staring at her. 'What a strange day this is turning out to be' she thought. 'At least I think it is day. Down here, it's hard to tell. Perhaps it's the middle of the night. Maybe I've gone forward in time... or backwards. Or maybe even sideways...'. She looked at her watch. It showed 15:00. 'That's odd... has my watch stopped? Didn't the tour start at three o'clock?' 'The rabbit did say you'd be back in no time' reminded the voice in her head.

The girl was brought back to her senses with a jolt. 'Your name... does it start with A?' demanded Rabbit. 'I'm not feeling quite myself... I can't seem to remember' she spluttered. 'Think, please... it's important' said White Rabbit urgently. 'Yes, do think' squawked the parrot who led the other creatures in the chorus 'Think... think... think...'. 'Quiet!' shouted the girl, 'I'm trying.' 'Very trying' said the mouse and ran under the seat. 'I know my name has five letters.' 'Write that down' said the dodo to the mouse. 'Five lettuces.' 'I know that three are vowels and two are consonants.' 'Write that down' said the dodo. 'Three trowels and two continents.' By now White Rabbit was jumping up and down, becoming more and more agitated. 'But tell us quickly, what are the letters?'

'Oh, I'm so muddled' said the girl. 'I think there's a C and an E... I'm sure there's an L...' 'Yes, what else?' 'There's an I.' 'And the last letter?' screamed the White Rabbit. 'I think it's an A! Yes, I'm sure it is!' she said.

Rabbit slumped down, disappointed. 'What does that spell, Dodo?' quacked the duck.' 'Let me see...' said Dodo, taking the five letters from Mouse. 'C E L I A... Celia! Write that down' said the dodo. 'What sort of name is that?' said the mouse. 'That' said Rabbit, 'is a very disappointing name.' 'It's a nice girl's name – I like it' said the turtle. At that point the train jolted to a sudden stop. And then slowly began to move... backwards... then forwards, then it jolted back again. 'I've never been backward in coming forward' she thought, but this was very unsettling.

The train jolted even more. The lights flashed on and off. The carriage shook violently. The White Rabbit hung on to the pole as the mouse slid past him down the carriage. The parrot flapped and squawked. 'Chaos, it's chaos! We're doomed!' Everything was suddenly upside down and jumbled up. Mouse's five letters whizzed around the ceiling, then began floating down and landed one by one on the floor, like leaves falling from a tree. 'Quick someone, stamp on those letters!' cried the White Rabbit. 'Quite right. I always put a stamp on my letters' thought the girl and giggled. Then as suddenly as it started, the train had stopped moving. The dodo trapped the pieces of paper with his feet. 'You could say now that the stationery is stationary' said her small voice. 'Quiet' said the girl.

The dodo lifted his feet. The letters lay on the floor in a line. 'That's better. And look!' said the White Rabbit as he bent over them 'Oh, my ears and whiskers! The letters... it's not C E L I A...' The letters had changed places. 'It's... I can hardly believe it... it's A L I C E!' 'That's what I said, didn't I?' whispered Alice. 'Or maybe not.'

'If your name is really Alice, might you be...' the White Rabbit paused '... the real Alice? Are you the Alice in the mirror? Are you the Alice from Mr Carroll's book? The Alice we've been waiting for?' Alice stood in front of the doors and looked at her reflection. 'I don't know, well, I suppose I might be' said the girl, rather startled. 'I know I was named after a character in *Alice in Wonderland* – and I'm sure my name is not Gryphon, or Bill.' She stared again at her reflection. There she was, wearing a frock. She had stripey socks and her hair was blonde, just like the Alice in the book. But she couldn't deny that it was also, without doubt, her. 'Somehow,' the dodo said, 'we appear to have two Alices in our midst – both ancient and modern. I do… do… don't know how…' At that moment, an advertisement burst onto the carriage's screen. *'For One Day Only! Special Offer – Buy One, Get One Free!'*

The rabbit leaped in the air. 'Oh my knees and elbows… you really are Alice!' Rabbit was staring at the reflection again. 'Do you see? Do you see? You are not just any old Alice, but *the* Alice!' Alice couldn't think what to say ('which makes a change' said her little voice).

Now the turtle went into his shell, the mouse did a somersault and the other creatures all started shouting at once. Parrot led the chant which grew louder and louder. 'Alice! Alice! She's come to rescue us!' Alice! Alice! She's come to rescue us'. Alice frowned. 'Hold on. What do you mean "rescue"?'

But the rabbit and the others drowned out her voice with their singing:

Twinkle, twinkle little girl,
How you've got us in a whirl.
Down below the world you are
Shining brightly like a star.

The White Rabbit fell to his knees. Then he jumped up and down again. Then he did a funny dance shouting 'Alice has come! You've come so we can have the adventure and... and... we can...'.

He rabbited on for five whole minutes – 'so much for saving time' thought Alice – his voice tailing off into jibberyibberish, which Alice thought was even more nonsense than the blathering her parents did. 'What funny behaviour' thought Alice. 'He seems to like my name even more than I do.' This was really becoming odder and odder.

By now White Rabbit was breathless. 'Oh my ears and whiskers... what a day this is going to be!' He'd pulled out his phone again. He leant across for a selfie with Alice. 'Say cheese.' 'Cheese!' interrupted Mouse.

'How rude! So much for being as quiet as a mouse' thought Alice. Rabbit was getting worked up, his cheeks had gone quite pink. 'Come on Alice, or we'll be late.' He was on his phone, texting. 'Late for what?' said Alice.

Rabbit began: 'We have to meet with the King. There's no time to delay. We must see him before "She" hears about this.' 'She?' queried Alice. Rabbit moved closer. 'The Queen' he whispered. He turned to the assembled creatures, flung out his arms and declared: 'Welcome everyone... to what I hope will be my last ever Great White Rabbit tour of the London Underground. And you, Alice, you are our special guest of honour.' The train started to glide out of the station. 'Victoria Line... two stops to King's Cross!' shouted Rabbit.

Warren Street to King's Cross

They were on the Victoria Line going north. Alice looked up at the boring map again. 'King's Cross. I wonder why he's cross?' she thought. 'I hope he won't be cross with me.' They all sat down. At least Alice sat, but the White Rabbit couldn't help but jump up from time to time and swing round the pole or hang from the straps in his excitement. The parrot was flapping up and down. Dodo, who was quite old, looked emotional. 'Do sit still, Mr Rabbit' said Alice. 'You're making me feel dizzy.' The rabbit lollopped down next to Alice. 'Why might this be your last ever tour?' asked Alice. But Rabbit wasn't paying attention.

'Oh my ears and whiskers!' said the rabbit as they pulled out of Euston Station. 'Next stop Wonderland!'

'No' corrected Alice. 'Next stop King's Cross. I'm good at reading maps you know.' Soon the voice in the train said *'The next stop will be King's Cross. Please mind the gap when stepping on to the platform.'* 'See?' said Alice 'I don't like to say I told you so but...'. 'Quite right' interrupted the White Rabbit. 'But it's time we told *you* something... a story... a story about a story. 'Oh, I like stories and riddles' thought Alice. 'Maybe this will be a good one that I can tell my sisters and Diana the cat when I get home.' The rabbit stood up. 'Are you sitting comfortably?' Just then the train braked suddenly and the rabbit shot forward. 'Well, *I'm* sitting comfortably' Alice laughed.

The train arrived at King's Cross station and they stepped out onto the platform. 'Let's sit here' said the White Rabbit. They sat on a bench under a huge Underground map. 'The thing is this...' began the rabbit... 'well, it's a bit complicated. I told the King about you and he's hurrying to meet us here. Ah, here comes the King now. He'll tell you the story better than I can.'

The King's story

There was a loud booming, panting kind of voice coming from down the platform. A man with a white beard dressed in the finest red gown was coming towards them along the platform. 'He looks just like the King in my set of playing cards' thought Alice. It was the Red King. 'Your Majesty.' The White Rabbit stood up and gestured to Alice to do the same. 'Your humble servant' said the rabbit bowing in front of the King.

They had to wait a minute for the King to get his breath back. Then he spoke in a deep gravelly voice. 'Great White Rabbit, my old bunny-buddy. I got your text… and have come… as soon as I could. The good thing is that I managed to sneak away without *Her* noticing. She's at the hairdresser's having her grey hairs dyed red again.' He smiled. 'And you must be Alice' said the King. 'My dear girl, we have waited a long time for you to arrive… a long, long time.' 'Pleased to meet you, your Majesty' said Alice, and she did the very best curtsey that she could manage. She smiled. 'That was the very best curtsey to royalty I've ever done', she thought. 'Well, of course it was…' said the small voice in her head 'as it's the only one you've ever done.' The King sat down, took a large red heart-shaped handkerchief out of his pocket and wiped his brow.

The King began. 'Alice – are you familiar with the book, *Alice in Wonderland*?' 'Of course' she said 'and I've seen all the films. My Mum and Dad loved the book so much they named me after the girl in the story.' 'And *Through the Looking Glass*?'. Alice nodded.

'Well, what people don't know is that there was once the start of a third Alice story.' 'What? How exciting!' exclaimed Alice. 'What was it called?' The Red King continued. 'It was set where we are now, in what was then the brand new London Underground. It was going to be called *Alice Goes Underground, Again*. But the problem for us is that the story was never finished. At the start of the story, some of us leave Wonderland on a day trip

to visit the new London Underground with the White Rabbit as our tour guide. Everyone is happy until the Queen of Hearts starts acting... well, you know...'. The King imitated the Queen's voice. 'Off with their heads!' 'What makes it worse is that the Duchess then joined her...' 'And she loves rabbit pie!' interrupted the White Rabbit. 'And Jack, the Knave of Hearts, has...' The King shivered at the thought. 'Jack has the Jabberwock, the JubJub Bird *and* the Bandersnatch under his control. And he uses them to frighten the rest of us.' 'But you are the King' said Alice. 'Can't you...?' 'No. I can't stop her. She's gone too far. I'm afraid we no longer see... what's the expression? Nose to nose.' 'I think you mean "eye to eye" said Alice helpfully as she watched a red tear roll down the King's cheek. 'Carry on, King' said Rabbit.

'Sorry, Rabbit. The problem is that the tale was never told to the end. So that's where the story stopped. We were left... forever stuck down here. In limbo.' 'In London' added Rabbit. The King continued: 'What we wanted was to go back home, to Wonderland. As the years went by, the Queen became more and more bossy.' 'She went completely off the rails!' interrupted Rabbit. The King went on: 'She took complete control. She bullied us all into obeying her commands. The Jack of Hearts trained up his Queen's Red Guards. She started spying on us, installing See-see TV in all the trains. She just loved being here, in the Underground, living in the shadows. We just want to go home, but without Alice, we can't. Rabbit says the idea was that a new Alice was supposed to come and help us escape back to Wonderland, but in the story Alice hadn't yet arrived. So, we Wonderland characters have been here ever since, under the Queen's thumb, or rather under Jack the Knave's boot, waiting for Alice... waiting... for you?' Alice was frowning. 'Alice, we need your help. We don't know how the story was meant to end, but what we do know is that we are trapped here and we desperately want to get back to Wonderland. The thing is...' He paused and took a deep breath.

'The thing is... Rabbit says that in the story Alice has A Plan... we hope that plan is to rescue us.' 'Only *you* can save us!' shouted the White Rabbit impatiently. 'Sorry, King.' The King continued. 'We think only *you* can defeat the Queen and her playing card Red Guards, outwit the Jabberwock and get us back to Wonderland, where we belong. We are relying on you... and your Plan.' He began reciting...

'You are young, darling Alice',
The Red King said
'We have waited for you for so long,
Yet you appear to be the right one,
Let us hope, dear girl, I'm not wrong.'

Alice turned to the rabbit. 'How do you know Alice is supposed to come and rescue you?' Rabbit answered: 'I am descended from the only Wonderland character that has ever been seen in your "real" world. Mr Carroll told this new Alice story to my great, great... great, great, great, great, great... great, great, great, ...' By now he'd run out of fingers and was taking off his shoes and socks so he could carry on counting on his toes. 'Phaw... what a paw pong!' said Alice holding her nose. 'I know a rabbit's foot is supposed to be lucky but...' 'Er... great... great...' the White Rabbit continued. 'That's enough of the greats!' interrupted the King, 'they're beginning to grate on me'. 'Sorry King.' Rabbit hopped on one foot.

'Mr Carroll told the tale to my ancestor in Oxford, the original White Rabbit, and it has been passed down through my family ever since. As has this – and he proudly held up his pocket watch. Of course it stopped at three o'clock years ago, but I still like looking at it.' 'You do have a rescue plan, don't you Alice?' said the King. 'A plan of escape back to Wonderland?' Alice tried not to look worried. She had no idea how she was supposed to get them back to Wonderland. 'I shouldn't tell a lie' she thought, 'so what shall I say? I know… a map is a kind of a plan isn't it? And I have the map that the White Rabbit gave me at the start of the tour.'

'Well, the thing is…' she said, feeling the map in her pocket. She paused. The creatures waited, holding their breath. 'I… I do have a plan.' The chant of 'Alice! Alice!' began again led by the parrot who had landed on her shoulder. Alice realized that they were relying on her. 'There's a lot resting on your shoulders' said the voice in her head, 'as well as a parrot'.

She turned to the King. 'The first thing in my plan is… is… we need to get everyone together and then… then I can tell you my idea for how we are going to escape.' 'Yippertydodo-dah!' shouted the White Rabbit, jumping up and down. 'Bipperty-dodo' said Dodo and the parrot flew off in circles squawking 'Bipperty, yipperty, bopperty-dodo.' 'We have complete faith in you, dear girl,' said the King. 'Now Rabbit, get on and text them all – The Hatter, the March Hare, the Mock Turtle, the Dormouse and all the others. The Hatter will be at Westminster – he likes it there as he says they are all mad so he fits in nicely. The Hare will no doubt be at his favourite Green Park; the Turtle is at Regent's Park; the others will be at stations around the Circle Line, so let me think… we'll meet in the middle. Tell them we are having a tea party. That won't raise any suspicion. Tell them to come to the *Drink Me! Eat Me!* café at Piccadilly Circus.' 'Oh, another circus' thought Alice. 'Maybe there will be clowns this time.' The King carried on. 'The Queen's Red Guard will be spying on your calls, so say nothing about…' he whispered… 'Alice…'. He looked around, as if he thought someone might be listening '…or Wonderland.'

The White Rabbit sent the text message speeding round the Underground system, to all the Wonderland characters. 'The plan is afoot!' shouted Rabbit. 'I hope it's longer than that' squeaked the mouse. They waited a while for the replies. For once there was silence. Rabbit was studying his phone. 'Everyone's replied except… no answer from the Dormouse.' 'He'll be asleep' said the King. 'You and Alice, please go and fetch him. Mouse, go with them. Dormouse will be at Bank Station. But be careful. Don't let the Red Guards see you. The rest of you, off you go to Piccadilly Circus. Order the tea and cakes. We mustn't let them know why we are meeting.' The King sat down exhausted on the platform seat. 'Aren't you coming?' asked Dodo. 'You go on without me' he replied. 'Leave me here. I'll be OK. I just need to rest a while. I'll join you soon.'

'As quick as you can' shouted Alice. 'You're all going five stops south on the Piccadilly Line.' 'The dark blue line' said Rabbit. He carried on: 'Alice, you and I are going direct to Bank, that's south on the Northern Line.' 'The black line' chipped in Alice, looking at her map as they scurried down the platform. 'See you at the café!'

TRACK SIX

Next stop Bank

Rabbit spoke. 'We are on the correct platform. Our Northern Line train is due in three minutes.' 'We are coming to wake you up, Dormouse' said Alice. 'Then,' said Rabbit, 'we must collect the King and get back to our friends before the Queen finds out.'

Alice was worried. The small voice in her head said 'You've promised that you can get them back to Wonderland. How are you actually planning to do that… actually?' 'Please be quiet little voice, I'm thinking.' 'I don't think you have any idea, do you?' interrupted the voice. 'I have until we get to Piccadilly Circus to think of something' thought Alice. The train arrived. '*Mind the gap!*' The White Rabbit sat down, watch in one hand, phone in the other, map on his knees. Alice even thought his ears were twitching as if they were picking up signals. 'I can track everyone's movements.' 'Did you say "track"?' laughed Alice. Rabbit wasn't listening. He looked at his phone again. 'OK. We now know that the Hatter has left Westminster. Everyone else is well on their way. And so are we.'

'He is definitely getting overexcited' thought Alice. 'He'll never sleep tonight.' 'This map is too small!' Rabbit declared, pulling another bigger fold-out one from his pocket. 'Still too small!' he said again, unfolding an even larger map which now covered nearly the whole carriage and buried the mouse under its sheets. Rabbit was now standing on the map, running up and down the train lines as he spoke in a breathless voice. 'They are all on their way to Piccadilly Circus... from Westminster – Circle line, change at Embankment. Green Park – one stop on the Piccadilly. Regent's Park – two stops south on the Bakerloo. But wait!' he shouted. He had collapsed exhausted onto a seat. 'We... we have to be clever... Remember what the King said. If the Queen finds out about you, Alice, she'll have Jack and his Guards out looking for us. We mustn't do anything... anything to risk them finding out that you are the real Alice. Not to mention the consequences...' he hesitated. 'Not to

mention the...'. 'You mean the Jabberwock!?' asked Alice 'We agreed not to mention it!' said the mouse sharply. They all trembled at the sound of the 'J' word. They fell quiet.

Alice was looking forward to the tea party with the Dormouse, the Mad Hatter and the March Hare. The tea party was her favourite part of her Alice book. Angel and Old Street stations came and went. Next stop Moorgate, then Bank. There was a small screen at the end of the carriage showing advertisements – for the *Drink Me! Eat Me!* café and the Great White Rabbit tour and the face of a smiling cat appeared advertising *The Cheshire Cats' Home.*

Then a bright red face suddenly appeared on the screen with red lips, red hair and bright red cheeks. And a voice, all too familiar to Rabbit and Mouse: '*The next stop will be Moorgate*' said the announcement. '*Mind the gap... mind the gap...*' There was a pause, then '*that is to say, the gap between your head and your shoulders! Ha ha ha ... off with their heads! Off with their heads!*'

At the sound of this chilling voice, the White Rabbit trembled again. 'It's the voice of the Queen of Hearts!

She has See-see TV in all the trains.' 'She can see inside the train?' 'You could say it's Tunnel Vision' said Alice's small voice. 'Take no notice of the Queen' said Rabbit. She's not looking at us, it's the way she likes to frighten everyone. Just keep your head down.'

The train stopped at Moorgate station. The doors opened and there, on the platform directly in front of them was just what Rabbit was hoping not to see – Jack with five of his Queen's Guards! All in red, menacing, their playing card bodies looking more like shields. Jack and the Red Card Guards stepped in to the carriage. 'Stay calm everyone' shouted Jack. 'This is just a routine check.' And the Guards started moving down the carriage.

Rabbit froze for a second then whispered, 'Say nothing Alice… keep your head down.' Mouse ran under the seat. One of the Guards approached them. 'Name?' he demanded. 'You know me,' said Rabbit, trying hard to keep calm and flashing his big white teeth in a smile. 'I'm White Rabbit.' 'And who is this?' demanded the guard. 'This? Who? Oh, this girl you mean?' stuttered Rabbit. 'Yes, this girl.' 'Er… this is… Celia. Sorry, got to go, this is our stop.'

The train came to a halt in Bank station. They moved quickly to the doors. And in that fraction of a second, before the doors opened, Jack caught sight of something… he was sure… in the reflection in the door, he saw, could it be?… the real Alice? The original Alice in a pinafore dress with long blonde hair? 'Alice… it's Alice! Get her!' he shouted to the nearest Guard. Too late. Rabbit and Alice had jumped off the train and the doors had closed. Rabbit and Alice were at Bank Station, while Jack and the Guards were already heading south to London Bridge. Alice turned her head to see Jack pressed against the door, beating his fists on the glass.

Alice and Rabbit looked up and down the platform. There was Dormouse, fast asleep on a bench. 'Dormouse!' Alice shouted, 'Quick, wake up!' Dormouse looked startled. 'H e l l o R a b b i t' he said sleepily. 'Who's your friend?' 'It's OK' said Rabbit. He whispered 'this is Alice. You must come with us, we have something important to tell you. Come on. Jack won't know where we are going. We must get to the café at Piccadilly Circus.' Rabbit was staring at the back of his hand. 'What are you doing Rabbit?' said Dormouse. 'I know the quickest way' declared Rabbit. Three stops on the Central Line to Holborn, then change and three stops south on the

Piccadilly Line.' 'Red and then dark blue' added Alice. 'Hurry, you two!' And off they rushed down the platform.

Rabbit stopped in his tracks. ('Not more puns!', said the little voice.) Rabbit seemed worried. 'Did you say "you two", Alice? Don't you mean "three"? Two and one makes three.' Rabbit had put his hands to his head. 'Everyone knows that' Alice said. 'This is no time for maths homework', she thought. 'Even you know that, don't you Dormouse?' But Dormouse didn't answer. He was asleep again. Rabbit picked Dormouse up and exclaimed, 'we should be three plus one equals four! Oh my cheese and chutney! We are missing one! Where's Mouse?'

Bank to Piccadilly Circus

Rabbit, Alice and Dormouse had arrived at Holborn and changed on to the Piccadilly Line and were now just leaving Leicester Square station. 'One more stop' said Rabbit. 'But what about Mouse?' said Alice. 'We've left him behind. He's still on the other train. What if the Guards get him?' 'I don't know. I can't think straight.' said Rabbit. 'He's tiny. Maybe they won't find him. We'll ask the King at the café. He'll know what to do.'

Meanwhile, on the southbound train, Jack and the Queen's Guards were looking for Mouse, who was hiding under a seat. 'Come out, come out wherever you are!' called Jack, looking under the seats, one by one. He stopped at one seat. At each one he said 'I think I smell a rat...'. This was too much for Mouse, who was

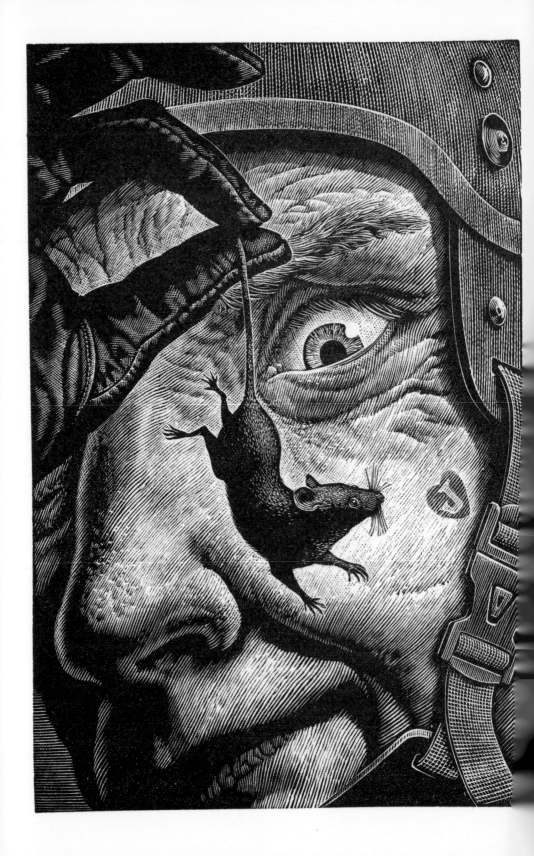

not going to stand for being called a rat. He jumped out from his hiding place. 'I'm no rat… I'm a mouse!' he shouted. Then, 'Ooops!' He'd given himself away. 'Get him!' commanded Jack, and Mouse was grabbed by one of the guards.

As their Northern Line train continued southwards Jack began to question Mouse. 'Now… tell me Mouse' he began in a soft, menacing voice, with a horrible grin on his face, 'tell me, who is that girl?' 'What girl?' said Mouse, trembling slightly. 'Let me help you remember' said Jack. And he held Mouse up by his tail. 'Oh, I do like tales. Do you by any chance have one to tell me?' Mouse wriggled but said nothing. 'Is her name really Celia… or might it be… Alice?' 'I'm not saying' said Mouse. 'The King said not to say anything.' 'The King?' Jack pressed his face close to the Mouse. 'Have you and Alice been talking to the King?'

At Piccadilly Circus, Rabbit, Alice and Dormouse had burst into the *Drink Me! Eat Me!* café. They were all there – the Hatter, the March Hare and everyone. The table was laid with tea and cakes and those around it were eating, drinking and laughing. They just thought they were there for a tea party. 'Quiet please!' shouted

Rabbit. 'May I introduce you to "The Real Alice".' There was dead silence. 'You don't need me to tell you that this is the day we have been waiting for all these years.' 'I thought he said he didn't need him to tell them,' thought Alice. Rabbit carried on. 'At last we can escape. Alice has A Plan!' There were loud cheers. 'A plan that will get us back to Wonderland without the Red Queen, without Jack and all their nasty Red Guards.' 'Hoorah!' they all shouted. 'Three chairs for Alice!' At which point three chairs were hurriedly placed for Alice to sit down on. 'You are our guest of honour, Alice' said Dodo. 'You must sit at the head of the table and chair the meeting.' 'I only need one chair, thank you,' said Alice, so Dormouse and Rabbit were invited to sit on the other two.

'Pleased to meet you, Alice' said the Hatter, 'You must have had a busy day. May I pour you some tea?' He picked up an enormous teapot. This is our own special brew.' 'Thank you' replied Alice. She thought how polite they were. 'Do you take milk?' 'Yes please.' 'How do you like it? Let's see. I can offer you a splash? A spot? A drop? Or a dash?' 'Can I have just a little?' said Alice. 'Sorry, that's not on the menu today.' Alice thought it was best not to argue. 'I'll have a dash then please.' 'Splendid choice. I love a dash,' said the Hatter, who

then dashed around the table three times, spilling all the milk everywhere.

'Delighted to make your acquaintance,' said the March Hare. 'May I offer you a cake? We make these ourselves. We call them mug cakes.' 'Don't you mean cupcakes?' 'Oh no,' said the Hare, 'these are much bigger. And they have a handle so you can pick them up more easily. What would you like? Would you like "lemon drizzle", "lemon downpour", "lemon cats and dogs" or "lemon violent storm with added thunder and lightning"? Sorry, we've sold out of "lemon spitting".'

Alice looked at the tea and cake. 'Be careful' said the voice in her head. The bottles of lemonade and the teapots all had labels on them that read 'Drink Me!' and the plates of cakes all said 'Eat Me!'. Alice remembered what happened in the Wonderland story when Alice ate and drank... 'Sorry, but I'm really not hungry right now and anyway we've no time for tea, we need to think what's happened to Mouse. He may have been captured by the Red Guards.' 'What do you think, King? Er... King?' It was only then that they all realized that the King wasn't there. 'We left him at King's Cross but he said he'd join us here,' said Rabbit. 'We must go back to King's Cross. He may be in trouble.' 'But they don't know about our meeting with the King or Alice's plan do... do... do they?' said Dodo.

The TV screen in the corner of the café flickered into life. *'I wouldn't be so sure of that!'* The Cheshire cat, or at least its smile came into view. It spoke. *'Attention! Be upstanding for your gracious Queen.'* Gradually, a large red face filled the screen. The voice pierced the air. *'Are you enjoying your tea and cake? Ha ha ha... off with your heads!'* 'Oh no, the Queen! How does she know we are here?!' asked Rabbit anxiously. 'The Queen is grinning from ear to ear, that's never a good sign' said the Hatter.

The Queen continued, *'White Rabbit... you made a Big Mistake. You really shouldn't have sent that selfie of you and Alice to the King. You should know that I have ways to check his phone. I saw the picture of you and the girl. I thought that was odd. Who could she possibly be? I told Jack to look at Dormouse's phone while he was asleep on Bank station. I saw you were all meeting at the café. I wondered why. And then... it all became clear when Jack told me he'd seen Alice, or at least her reflection. The real Alice. And you think you have a plan and are going to escape back to Wonderland? Ha ha ha! Never!'*

'How do you know about that?' cried Rabbit at the screen. *'Well… let's say a little bird told us. Or rather… a little mouse.'* 'You have Mouse?' said Dodo. 'Don't you dare hurt him. If you so much as hurt a whisker on his head, I'll…' *'You'll what!?'* interrupted the Queen, laughing. *'And by the way, I know that the King isn't with you. I'll be dealing with him later… or rather my Guards will. Be warned!'* And the screen went black.

'Where is the King?' asked Alice. Rabbit was staring at his phone. 'Can you get his position Rabbit? We must find him.' Rabbit stamped his feet. 'They're blocking my signals. I can't locate him. His phone is on but he's not answering.' 'Is he still at King's Cross?' asked Dodo. 'Give me that phone, quick,' said March Hare. 'I'm calling the King's number again.' 'But that doesn't work' said Alice. 'Hold on,' said Hare and he put the phone close to his huge ear. 'My hearing is second to none. Quiet everyone. I can hear… the sound of a train coming through the King's phone. I can hear an announcer. He's saying *"The… next … stop… will be… Queensway"*. The King has been captured. They must be taking him to the Underground bunker at Queensway!' 'We have to rescue him!' cried Alice. 'Hold on, Alice,' said the Hatter. 'What about the plan to escape? Alice, tell us. What is your plan?' Alice hesitated... she didn't have a plan. What could she say? Dodo cut in. 'That will have to wait – Alice can tell us later. First things first. We must rescue the King. Now Rabbit – how do we get to Queensway from here?' 'It's a doddle, Dodo' Alice interrupted. 'Piccadilly to Green Park, change to the Jubilee going north to Bond Street... then three stops on the Central west to Queensway.' 'Why not Bakerloo to Oxford Circus and then onto the Central Line?' said Rabbit. 'Too risky' replied Alice. 'They might be expecting me at Oxford Circus.' 'Good point' said Rabbit as he pointed the way to the platform. 'Good point' thought Alice. 'Let's go.' As they rushed out of the café to catch the train, Alice saw that Rabbit was on his phone again. 'Who are you calling?' 'If we play our cards right, we might just get some help...'.

Piccadilly Circus to Queensway

They were on the Central Line, coming in to Queensway Station. They were all nervous. What would they find? Would the Guards be there, and the Queen? What about the terrible Jack and his Jabb…? And had they got the King? Rabbit was peering out of the window as the train slowed. 'Oh no!' he exclaimed. 'I can see the Queen's Guards. I can see the Queen and Jack the Knave. But I can't see the King.'

They jumped from the train onto the platform. They had been feeling brave. They had been sure that they could rescue the King. Now they weren't so sure.

Five Queen's Guards were lined up facing Alice and the others on the platform. Alice looked at Rabbit. He'd gone even whiter than ever. The Hatter had pulled his hat down over his eyes. She turned to look at him. He was trembling. His teeth were chattering. 'Do you think he has false teeth?' said Alice's voice in her head. 'Shush!' said Alice, 'there's a time to talk about teeth and this is not it!' 'What time would it be good to talk about teeth?' asked the voice. 'Two-thirty of course' said Alice under her breath, 'now please be quiet.'

The Red Guards stood aside to allow the Queen of Hearts to step forward, followed by Jack. 'Where's the King?' shouted Rabbit. 'We demand you let him go.' 'That's no way to address a Queen' said the Queen calmly. 'It's very rude of you.' Suddenly her voice changed. 'You are in no position to demand anything!' she shouted. 'The King is being… shall we say, cared for, by the Duchess and he's going nowhere… and neither are you! Ha ha ha! You're never going back to Wonderland. The girl can't save you now.'

'You let the King go now!' shouted Alice as she stepped in front of the group.' 'Well, well' said the Queen. 'You are not slow in coming forward. And we haven't even been formally introduced. I am the Queen. I rule the Underground and no-one is going anywhere.' 'You can stay if you like but we are going to Wonderland,' said Rabbit, 'and Alice is going to take us there. She has a plan!' 'Ha ha ha!' laughed the Queen in a terrifying mocking voice. 'You have no plan.' 'Oh yes I have!' retorted Alice as she took another step towards the Guards. 'Have you really?' said the small voice in her head. 'Well… I have the map.'

'Queen's Red Guards! Attention!' shouted Jack. 'Seize the girl!' commanded the Queen. 'Off with her head!' The Guards leapt forward to grab her, at which point Parrot swooped down and pecked at one Guard. Hare leapt up and with his huge back feet, kicked another that was squashed flat – well even flatter – by Turtle, who had been knocked over in the commotion. 'Who's holding all the cards now, Jack?' Turtle mocked. But then Dodo shouted 'look out behind you!'

They turned to see another pack of Guards marching down the platform. In their bright red uniforms they looked a fearful sight. 'Oh no,' muttered the Hatter, 'we are cornered. We are trapped in the middle.' 'We're do…do…doomed' stammered Dodo. But Rabbit was jumping in delight. The new Guards stood to attention and their leader, the Ace of Hearts, stepped forward.

'We received your message, Rabbit, and we are at your service. Everyone, may I introduce you to the *King's* Red Guards. We hold allegiance to the King. If the King is in trouble, we will fight to protect him. I repeat, we are the King's Guards, *not* the Queen's. We have been carrying out the Queen's evil doing for long enough. We've been waiting for this moment, the moment when Alice came. We are here to protect you.'

Alice, Rabbit and the others stepped aside. The five King's Guards were now lined up facing the five Queen's Guards. Ace stepped forward. 'Your Majesty. In the tradition of battles fought by generations of Card Guards, this fight must be settled by Carroll's Ancient Rules for Disagreements. Failure to respect the rules of this card game will automatically forfeit all power. If you wish to continue as Queen, you have no choice. Win the game and you can take Alice.' There was a gasp from Rabbit and the others. 'Lose the game and you will surrender the King.'

'Oh my goodness' thought Alice. 'This doesn't sound like a card game to me. I don't remember capturing anyone when I play Snap with my sisters.' The Queen and Jack were clearly shocked. Never before had they been forced into a contest for their right to rule. The Queen's face went redder and redder as she tried to spit out the words of protest. But she couldn't. Finally, all she could muster was 'All right! Play the Game! We will settle this now. I have no doubt that my Guards will win. And when I have won... off with their heads!' And she pointed at Alice and the others in defiance.

Alice and Rabbit watched open mouthed. 'What are the rules?' asked Alice. Dodo spoke. 'None of us have ever seen the game played out. Never in the history of Wonderland has anyone challenged the Queen in this way. The game is played with the ten number cards in a suit.' 'In a suit of armour, preferably' thought Alice. Rabbit carried on. 'In this case the Ace to ten of hearts. Each side plays a card in turn. The higher number wins, and the losing card falls to the floor.' Dodo continued. 'The side with the most cards standing at the end is the winning team, at which point the losers are defeated and must surrender.'

The card game of life and death began. The cards shuffled their feet and jumbled up their positions, turning their backs on their opponents. Now each side couldn't see the number on the front of the opposing cards.

Jack spoke. 'By Carroll's Ancient Rules, on the shout of "Turn", the first pair will turn to face each other. We shall repeat that five times until we have a victor.'

'Turn!' The first two in the line spun round to face each other. 'Queen's Card 6 beats King's Card 5' and the 5 Card fell flat to the floor. '1-0 to the Queen.' 'See,' shouted the Queen 'I knew we'd win.'

'Turn!' yelled Jack. The second pair spun round. 'King's Card 3 beats Queen's Card 2. That's 1-1.' Cheers from Alice's side as the 2 Card fell flat.

'Turn! Queen's Card 8 beats King's Card 4. 2-1 to the Queen.' Card 4 fell down. There was a groan from Dodo. The Hatter had his hat over his eyes again. Even Dormouse was wide awake. 'I can't sleep, I can't sleep with all this excitement' he said.

Again, Jack called out. 'Turn! King's Card 10 beats Queen's Card 9. It's 2-2 and it's all on the final pair.'

'I can't stand the tension, Rabbit' said Alice. 'It's OK' replied Rabbit brightly. 'We know that the last card must be the Ace as he hasn't faced them yet. So we are bound to win.' It took all his self-control not to start jumping up and down in delight.

Jack spoke. 'This is the last pairing. Whoever has the higher number will win. Turn!' The last two cards turned to face each other. Just as Rabbit had said, the King's card was the Ace. 'We've won!' shouted Alice. Jack shouted even louder. 'Queen's Card 7 beats King's Card 1! I declare the Queen the winner, 3-2. Alice comes with us.'

For a second there was silence. 'You are the loser, Ace! Fall to the floor!' cried the Queen. And Jack moved forward to grab Alice. But Ace stepped in front of him. 'Cheat!' shouted Ace. 'We are playing by Carroll's Ancient Rules and it says quite clearly...' He pulled a small booklet out of his pocket. It was an old battered notebook. He held it up and waved it triumphantly. 'I have it here... in Mr Carroll's own handwriting. Rule 7, sub-section 3, sub-sub-section 'd'.' He read 'An Ace trumps any other number! *We* are the winners 3-2! Fall to the floor, Card 7. I insist that you release the King.' Parrot led the chant. 'Free the King! Free the King...'.

Then, appearing, out of the shadows at the end of the

platform came the Duchess, running with the King. 'Quick, King' said the Duchess, 'go to your friends.' The King joined the group while the Duchess turned on the Queen and Jack. 'I cannot carry on. This is the last straw. The Ancient Rules must be obeyed. You have cheated!' The Queen looked even more shocked. For a second she forgot about Alice and turned her anger on the Duchess. 'Grab her. Lock her up!'

This command unleashed all kinds of pandemonium but even above all the shouting, Hare's big ears could pick up the sound of Jack on his phone... 'I can hear him' he said to himself, 'he's saying "Release the J... Release the Jabb...".'

Alice could hear something too – a kind of 'whoosh' coming closer. 'What's that noise?' said Alice to Rabbit. 'It's just a train coming through the tunnel.' He looked at his watch and his timetable. 'It will be the 3 o'clock Central Line train to Ealing Broadway.' 'No, Rabbit' said Dodo, as the low rumbling sound grew louder and louder, as it drew nearer.

'Oh my ears, paws and whiskers! It's not a train. It's the... Jabberwock!'

They all ran to the end of the platform. The Jabberwock burst out of the tunnel into the station, filling the width of the track. It was gaining on them. 'Run! Come on King, keep up!' They rushed through an exit and down the corridor. 'To the next platform! Quick!' The Jabberwock was snapping its jaws, but it was so big its wings were catching on the corridor walls. Down the stairs, round the corner, they ran on to the platform, the Jabberwock close behind. A train was just arriving at the platform. 'Jump on,' shouted Rabbit. But the Jabberwock had managed to stick his head into the carriage and the doors now closed on the Jabberwock's neck. They opened and closed on his neck again… and again. 'Off with his head!' called out the Hatter. The Jabberwock pulled out his head and the train sped away. They all slumped onto the seats.

It was Dodo who spoke first, out of breath. 'We've defeated the Guards, we've escaped from Jack and the Queen, we've rescued the King and seen off the Jabberwock… for now at least. What do we do now, Alice?' Alice didn't know what to say. If only she had a plan to help them escape back to Wonderland. 'Think, think' said the voice in her head.

TRACK NINE

Queensway to Oxford Circus

'The plan, the plan, what's the plan?' they all demanded at once. Rabbit spoke up amongst the hubbub. 'Alice must be exhausted. Leave her be and let her rest a while.' Alice sat quietly, looking at her map. She'd been going round and round. So much so that she wondered if she would ever stop moving. Where was she? Where was she going now? In fact she began to wonder if this was really happening. 'Concentrate' she told herself. She got out her map. 'We've just left Lancaster Gate' she thought. 'OK. I know where I am.'

By now the train was at Bond Street going east on the Central Line. Alice stared at the map. 'How very odd' she thought. 'How very, very, very, very... odd. It looks different.' She folded it up. Maybe she was mistaken.

She opened it again and focused on it more closely. No, she wasn't seeing things. Or rather 'I *am* seeing things!' Now, she was feeling more excited than she could ever remember. At this moment she thought no one in the whole world could be more excited. She jumped to her feet. 'Everybody…' She was trying to speak calmly. 'Everybody – I think we are safe for a while. We need to get off at Oxford Circus.' Just then the automated voice announced *'The next stop will be Oxford Circus. Please mind the MAP when stepping on to the platform.'* 'Did they say 'map'?' said Rabbit.

Dodo held the door open and looked both ways. 'All clear' he called and the tour party staggered on to the platform. 'The Queen will still be after us. She'll be training up a new set of Guards to come looking for Alice' said Hatter. 'Not to mention the Jabb…' 'You said not to mention it!' barked Rabbit.

'Sit down here, King.' Rabbit led the King to a bench on the platform. Above his head was a very large Underground map. All the various train lines in beautiful colours; every line drawn either horizontal, vertical or diagonal. A masterpiece of design. All the characters – the Hatter, the March Hare, the Dodo, the

White Rabbit – and all the creatures gathered round facing Alice, who stood in front of them. 'I am delighted to tell you...' began Alice, putting on her best formal voice, 'I am delighted to tell you that I have A Plan.' 'You could call it Plan A, A for Alice' said her small voice. Alice continued: 'I can now explain how you will all escape the Queen and the Underground world and can finish the story by returning to Wonderland.'

There was excited cheering from the group. Alice raised her voice. 'Rabbit – do you remember when we first met? Do you remember telling me about all the train lines that criss-crossed London?' 'Of course,' said Rabbit. 'I was going to take you on a guided tour.'

'Well,' said Alice, 'I did agree that it was a brilliant map, but when you were listing all the stations on the Victoria Line, I must admit, I thought it was a bit boring. Remember, I said "will this never end?" and you replied "yes, at Walthamstow Central"?' 'I remember' said Rabbit, and everyone laughed. 'Well,' she continued, 'remind me... what is after Walthamstow Central on the Victoria Line, or Harrow on the Bakerloo, or Upminster on the District, or Morden on the Northern Line, or Cockfosters on the Piccadilly and all the other last stations?' 'Er, nothing' said Rabbit. 'It's the end of the Underground world.' 'Not any more!' declared Alice with a huge smile on her face. 'Look behind you.'

In the reflection in the glass covering the big map, they could see the real Alice, in her pinafore dress, with blonde hair and stripey socks. Alice was holding up her small map. 'We can see Alice holding a map' said Dodo. 'Yes' said Alice. 'But look now...' Something very odd started happening. First, the title at the top of the big map changed from 'Underground' to 'Wonderground'. Then the spot for Oxford Circus station began to glow bright red and pulsate like a flashing light. An arrow appeared and the words *'You Are Here'*. Then, the blue Victoria Line that used to stop at Walthamstow began growing longer, travelling on to a new stop. An extra stop. The brown Bakerloo was also moving beyond Harrow to an extra stop. There was a new station appearing after Upminster on the green District Line. All round the edges of the map were new stations, all glowing in coloured neon light. At the end of every line was a brand-new station – and the new stations all had the same name! 'Wonderland!' exclaimed Rabbit. 'All lines now go to Wonderland!' shouted Dodo. The chanting began... 'We're coming home!'

'Oh my ears and whiskers!' said Rabbit. 'Oh, upon my hat!' said the Hatter. 'Upon my even bigger ears and whiskers' said Hare. 'Oh... I do... do... don't believe it!' said Dodo. And the others all saw the same thing and began dancing and cheering. Rabbit was so excited. 'Every line has an extra stop – every coloured line carries on to an extra station called Wonderland. Walthamstow isn't the end of the world anymore. Nor is Harrow, or Morden or any of the others.'

Alice spoke calmly. 'I believe if you get a train to the end of any of these coloured lines, it will take you all to Wonderland. You are all going home. Is everybody ready for the trip of a lifetime?' They all hugged each other. 'We must hurry. There's no doubt that the Queen and Jack and the J... will still be after us and there will be more Guards looking for me. So, this is what we must do. You have to split up – they can't follow you all. Split into small groups and each take a different route home. Agreed?' 'Agreed!' they all replied.

They looked again at the big map on the wall. 'OK' said Alice. 'We are at Oxford Circus. We need to get to the Wonderland stations as quickly as possible. March Hare and Mad Hatter – you take the Bakerloo

Line north past Harrow & Wealdstone to Wonderland.' As she spoke the line on the map lit up. 'Parrot and the creatures – you take the blue Victoria Line past Walthamstow Central and on to Wonderland.' Their route lit up on the map. 'The King and Dormouse – the red Central Line, change at Tottenham Court Road onto the black Northern Line, south past Morden to Wonderland. Dodo, you take Mouse with you – brown Bakerloo south, change at Embankment, green District Line past Upminster to Wonderland.' By now everyone was happy and excited but Dodo was looking worried. 'What's wrong, Dodo?' asked Alice. 'You said for me to go with Mouse. Where is Mouse? Oh no! Remember – he was captured by the Guards. We haven't seen him since.' The King stepped forward. 'It's all fine' he said. 'Sorry, I should have mentioned it before. The Duchess slipped him in my pocket when she let me go. I've just felt him wriggling to escape!' and he pulled Mouse out of his pocket. 'Thanks, King' squeaked Mouse. Now they were all together again.

'Rabbit – what do you think?' asked Alice. 'Which way will you go?' 'You and I can go two stops on the Central, change at Holborn and zoom north, through Cockfosters to Wonderland!' he replied. 'Sorry,' said

Alice, 'you said "you and I". I can't go with you. I must get back to my home, back to Oxford.'

Rabbit was about to say something, perhaps to try and persuade Alice to go with them, when a train pulled up at the platform and out jumped Jack and more Guards… and the Queen. 'And what's that?' shouted Dodo, pointing at a huge, ugly bird that was flapping down the platform. 'That's the Jub-jub bird' said the King. 'It's been let out of its cage! That means big trouble. No one, not even Jack, can control the Jub-jub bird. It's vicious and will eat anything…' 'Or anyone!' added Rabbit in a scared voice. 'Quick, everyone, split up – run to your platforms' shouted Alice. 'No, no… it's too late, they'll catch us' shouted Rabbit even louder. 'Follow me!'

Rabbit had been a guide on the Underground for years. 'I know every last nook and cranny.' 'Crook and Granny?' said Dodo. 'Has he gone mad?' 'Nothing wrong with that' said the Hatter, as they charged along a narrow corridor. 'In here, quick' ordered Rabbit as he opened a door with a huge key. 'It leads to one of the old tunnels that isn't used anymore.' They squeezed inside, shut the door and waited. It was pitch black. There was just one small window above the door.

'Parrot,' said Alice, 'take Mouse and fly up and tell us what you can see.' Parrot squawked 'Jack and the Guards, Jack and the Guards. They've stopped. Stopped. They're looking around, not knowing which way to go, way to go, way to go.' 'What about the Jub-jub bird?' asked Hatter. Mouse crooked his neck to see. 'The Jub-jub has arrived.' Then there was the most terrifying scream. 'The bird is angry... very angry... and very hungry' Mouse squealed. 'The Jub-Jub is attacking the Guards! They are scattering. He's picked up Jack in his mouth and is flying away down the corridor! The Queen is running for her life!'

There was cheering in the small dark room. 'Shush' said Rabbit, 'they might hear us.' 'I don't think they'll hear anything, with the noise Jack and the Queen are making themselves' said Alice, giggling. They waited... gradually the sound of their screams faded away. Then silence. Rabbit opened the door just a crack. He put his finger to his lips and peeped out. He twitched his nose. 'All clear' he said, and one by one they came out slowly into the light.

'Right,' said Alice, 'Now, you really must all get going. You remember your routes. Keep a lookout out for any more Red Guards. Go as fast as you can now.' 'Goodbye Alice' said the King, 'and thank you. We will never forget you,' he and Dodo shouted as they disappeared with the others down the corridor. They all ran off in different directions, down different corridors towards different platforms, to catch their trains. 'The trains all leave at 3 o'clock!' shouted White Rabbit, looking at his watch.

'See you all in Wonderland!'

Oxford Circus and Home

'You must go now as well' said Alice to Rabbit. 'Goodbye Alice. I hope we'll meet again.' They hugged each other. Rabbit slipped something into Alice's pocket. Then he turned and ran off, waving back to her. 'Maybe I'll come to Oxford one day' he called back as he ran. 'You can show me the rabbit hole that my grandfather disappeared down. My great, great, great, great…' The 'greats' became more and more distant till they faded away. Now Alice was standing at the foot of those funny moving stairs. 'Last time I was here, they were going down. But not now. "What goes down must come up". Isn't that what they say?' Alice was still a bit confused. It seemed like such a long time ago that she was there. She glanced at her reflection. For the last time, she saw herself in that beautiful dress. 'Goodbye Alice… goodbye,' she whispered.

As she stepped onto the stairs, she noticed a sign: 'Rabbits must be carried on the escalator'. 'Oh,' she thought, 'how silly. Not everybody can be expected to have a rabbit with them.' She started moving up. At the top of the escalator, she remembered that she had an Oyster card. She slapped it down. 'Careful!' came the voice of the Oyster, 'please be gentle.' And then it spoke:

> *'Thank you, thanks for taking us,*
> *we've loved to show you round*
> *Thank you, thanks for helping them,*
> *to escape the Underground*
> *We tried to tell them more than once,*
> *that one day you'd be found.'*

She could see a shaft of sunlight. There was noise all around. There were people hurrying and scurrying. There were tourists, people going to work, crisscrossing in all directions. The stairs took her up and up and she was finally back at the top... in Oxford Street. 'Oh, there you are,' said Alice's older sister. 'I couldn't see you for a moment.' 'What time is it?' asked Alice. 'It's just gone 3 o'clock. Come on, time to go home, I think. We need to get the bus back to Paddington. Sorry if it's been a boring day for you, Alice.'

For once, Alice didn't know what to say.

On the train home, Alice fell asleep. She woke up just as she heard the announcer say, '*The next stop will be Oxford. Oxford will be the final station stop.*' Memories tumbled into her head. Rabbit… rescuing the King… defeating the Jabberwock… Or had it all been a dream? She felt in her pocket. Maybe not. She pulled out a crumpled Underground map. A piece of paper fell to the floor. 'What's that?' said her sister. Alice picked it up. It was Great White Rabbit's return ticket from Wonderland to London. She turned the ticket over. On the back, written in tiny rabbit writing, was this: 'Answer to joke: at a whale-weigh station'. How curious. 'How very, very odd' said the voice in her head.

Meanwhile, in Wonderland, the King and all the characters were safely arriving home too. All except Rabbit… The King was reading a message he'd just received from him. '*Sorry not to join you but I'm sure I'll be visiting you soon… as soon as I can get away.*' 'Rabbit is in danger!' shouted the King. He carried on reading Rabbit's message. '*I shouldn't have changed my route. They were waiting for me. At Warren Street station, a pack of Red Guards boarded the train. I managed to jump off just before the doors closed which left some on the train. The rest chased me down the corridor. A good job I know all the nooks and crannies. I've told you that it's a warren down there. I've got all I need – lots of lettuce, my timetables, very great grandfather's pocket-watch and of course the memories of a magical day. I'll lie low for a while. They won't find me. Love GWR.'*

'We must go and rescue him' called Hare. 'Do... do... don't worry. He'll be ok' said Dodo. 'I think. Yes, I'm sure he will.' If I know my old bunny-buddy, they'll never track him down.

They sat down for tea, cakes and a toast. The King, Hare, Dodo, Dormouse and all. King lifted up his cup. 'Alice will be home in Oxford now. A toast' he cried, 'to both Alices, old and new!' Everyone lifted their cups and joined in. 'To Alice!' 'To Alice!' Everyone but Dormouse, who was of course, fast asleep.

Was this the end of the story, I wonder?

Alice's Underground Portfolio

We hope you have enjoyed this book and
Andrew Davidson's wonderful illustrations.
They are wood engravings, produced by cutting into
the top surface of endgrain boxwood blocks. Being
very slow growing, the rings are tightly packed,
enabling the engraver to cut with small, sharp, metal
tools in any direction without snagging. This was the
common way to illustrate publications throughout the
19th century. Among the most famous were for
Alice in Wonderland and *Alice through the Looking-glass,*
originally drawn by John Tenniel, but then engraved
by the firm of the Dalziel Brothers.

Alice's Underground Portfolio consists of a limited
edition, signed set of the wood engravings, printed
direct from the blocks, plus accompanying booklet.

For more information, please contact:
peter.a.lawrence@btinternet.com